No Other Reason

EL HOFFMAN

As my Grandpa always said,
"No day will ever go exactly how you expected it to when you woke up in the morning."

AUTHOR'S NOTE

This book includes an original poem by Pat Ulacco, used with his permission. His likeness is also referenced with consent. His work appears with full credit, and he retains all rights to the poem.

REPRESENTATION NOTE

No Other Reason features an autistic, bisexual protagonist.

PRAISE FOR *NO OTHER REASON*

"Sweet, nostalgic, and full of quiet longing, No Other Reason is a cozy, no-spice friends-to-lovers gem that proves sometimes the right person was in your life all along—perfect for fans of slow-burn romance with heart and humor."

— NEWINBOOKS

CONTENT NOTE

No Other Reason is classified as a new adult contemporary romance and contains references to mental health, mild sexual suggestiveness, and one brief, non-graphic instance of inappropriate sexual behavior by a secondary character.

"Tales of a Borderline Romantic"

Taking a magnifying glass to every interaction
But me desperate for clues
Is nothing new

Part One

O n this Thursday in April, I get off from my job as a legal assistant at a high-end law firm in Charleston, South Carolina. Upon exiting the building and pulling my phone out of my purse, I notice a notification from my long-distance friend Stephan.

"Breathe, Phoebe. You are Phoebe Johnson, you can handle this," I say to myself.

Opening the notification, I notice that he liked my newest selfie on Facebook. A like, not a heart react, but he seems to have done it within minutes of my posting it. I thought I looked great, wearing a burnt orange autumnal dress with a black cardigan and grey boots. I even had a sterling necklace I received as a Christmas gift from my mother a few years back. "Why a like and not a heart?" I think to myself.

Driving home, I was still mentally rolling my eyes from a conversation I had had with Owen, one of the interns in my office. He's a 20-year-old who thinks he is better than everyone with his unrealistic sense of superiority. He essentially cosplays as a student, mentioning that he had dropped out of 7 separate schools and is technically enrolled in another, yet hadn't taken any classes in two years. "I'm just too smart for school, you know? I'm self-taught, and my grandparents taught me about life. I'm very mature for 20, so you should go out with me sometime, and I can prove it to you," he said one day.

During that conversation, and in every other one I have with him, I picture him holding up a monocle and acting in a community theater play set in the 1800s. Many times that I speak to him, it seems like he wants me to pity him. Owen just wants the credit of being a student without doing any of the work.

Meanwhile, I am almost finished preparing for my Bar Exam and will be a full-fledged lawyer soon, perhaps even partner someday. Once I get home from work, I choose to stop wasting my time dwelling on my coworker. My thoughts drift back to my friend Stephan. "I read way too far into every word you say," I say aloud to myself, while twirling my chest-length, wavy blonde hair in front of the entryway mirror.

You once said to me, "I wish that my family hadn't moved away when we were kids. I still wonder what could have happened."

Who says things like that to their opposite sex friend? You like my stories on Instagram and my TikToks, but is it just surface level? Auto pilot? Am I overthinking things?

The next morning, after drinking a cup of coffee, I pull up your TikTok again to look at the few videos you've posted of yourself. You uploaded ones of you just talking, some of you painting or drawing, and other random ones that happen to show more of your face. Your smile is so cute in such a dorky way, yet you don't know how I feel about you. I often find my thoughts drifting off to your so-dark-brown-it's-almost-black hair and your sharp, ice blue eyes. I normally only fall for brown, green, and hazel, but there is just something about your eyes. If only we had gone to the same high school, I would've voted for you in the "nicest eyes" category. Mara Johnson had to win, though, with her yellow-green, catlike eyes. So unique. Meanwhile, mine are merely an iridescent brown.

For a moment, I find myself grateful that you've never posted a picture or video with another woman. Within a few seconds, I notice you viewed my profile too. "Is this a sign?" I think to myself, while continuing to twirl my hair. "I really care about you, and I hope you're doing well," I message him with no context. "I care about you, too," he responds. He then likes a few stories on my Instagram. Whenever this happens, I become so ecstatic that I nearly lose touch with reality.

We have some back-and-forth conversations from time to time, but never enough to convince me that he likes me. He never compliments me, but he talks about random things he is up to and expresses care and interest in the things I do. All potential signs of interest.

Later that day, I go to work and research the legalities of mold in a just-purchased home, as well as the timeframe allotted for backing out of a contract in South Carolina. One of the partners at my firm has a strong case and needs to ensure the legal precedent is accurate and airtight.

I do a grueling day of work, preparing a large document with all of my notes and research, and while I love it,

I am greatly looking forward to dealing with actual lawsuits and litigation, rather than notetaking, researching, or tagging along "for experience." I just need to pass my Bar Exam. It's also difficult to focus on work when I daydream about a man who probably doesn't like me or even know that I like him. There are so many songs and other media about unrequited love for a reason!

* * *

5 pm, clock out time. I close my laptop and zip it up within its case before putting it in my shoulder bag. I shrug on my green cardigan, the one I bought on that trip to Brooklyn a few years back.

I have a date tonight with a local accountant that I met on a dating app the other day. I'm not terribly excited, but I can't hold out hope that the guy I have starry eyes for will ever feel the same, or that I'll ever see him again. His family had moved to West Texas during the summer after kindergarten, and while we had reconnected on social media later in life, Texas had felt like a world away from South Carolina when I was younger.

My date, Bryan, and I have dinner plans at a local Basque restaurant, and I have my eyes on a cod dish with chunks of garlic on top. I meet up with him, and on paper he would be a great match, but I don't live on paper. He's tall but not too tall, with brown hair, brown eyes, and a bit of nicely presentable facial hair. We have a good conversation, and he is clearly well educated and intelligent, given that he has a CPA. But again, I don't live on paper.

He compliments my eyebrow piercing, which I appreciate as it's a bit of an unusual adornment in my profession. 14k solid white gold, custom fitted to my face.

I tell him that his eyes are some of the nicest I have ever seen, truly sparkly. I just didn't feel a spark with our conversation like I noticed in his eyes, and I don't feel the potential of any love with him. After our family style dinner, where I hogged the fries, he proposes a walk on the beach. I acquiesce, as sometimes you don't feel something until later during a date or even until the second date, but despite our conversation about having been to some of the same concerts and both preferring blondies to brownies, I just can't see myself marrying this guy. At the end of the date, he leans in to kiss me, and I turn away. He ends up kissing me on the cheek, and I try to suppress a gag. I had gone out with, dated, and been involved with other men and a few women over the years, but ever since reconnecting with Stephan on social media, it has felt like a waste of time and breath. I can't tell him I feel that way, though.

That night, I sent Stephan a long message that I would prefer not to remember. I am grateful that I didn't have alcohol clouding my judgment, but despite not telling him I liked him specifically, I still felt embarrassed at being more vulnerable than I would care to be during daylight hours. After he heart reacted the message but didn't respond, I noticed that he had posted a picture of a peanut butter and jelly sandwich with potato chips inside on his story. That was my sandwich idea. I had taught him how to make that when we were in kindergarten, and I still eat them weekly, preferably with strawberry or cherry jam or jelly.

*　*　*

Two weeks later, my coworker Katarina is giving a presentation on a new law that was just passed in our jurisdiction and how it could affect some of the local cases we are working on, when my phone buzzes three times in quick succession. Stephan said he just booked an art showing in North Charleston for the following month, and he was wondering if he could stay with me as he lived the starving artist life, followed up by a "haha jk" in true internet fashion.

"Just kidding, to which part?"

"I'm not a starving artist, but I would love to stay with you if you'd have me."

I respond immediately with confirmation but have to suppress the urge to show anything other than friendly excitement. Then I choose to put my phone away, needing to stay professional in the workplace if I have any hope of getting made partner.

After I walk out of the steel and glass building at 5 pm, I start typing and deleting and typing and deleting the words "I like you..." hoping he would ask me what I kept trying to say or say something like "I can see you typing," but after realizing I wasn't ready to admit my feelings, I stopped doing this little ritual.

One month: the countdown starts now. I still remember that when we were little kids, his older sister Clara had hugged me and said that she felt I was a sister of hers as well. Looking back at that moment, I had always wanted to marry into her family. I just felt that Stephan and I had never had the chance.

After dinner, I call my mother and ask, "Do you remember Stephan Hale?"

"Of course, I remember Stephan! He was your first crush. Why? Is he getting married or something? Oh, honey…I know what that feels like."

"What? No! He's coming to visit Charleston, and I'm anxious."

"Of what, honey? Oh, you're in love with him…aren't you?"

"You basically just asked the same thing twice, but in different words. He's just a friend, Mom," I say. "A very male friend. Who I haven't seen in twenty years."

"Riiiiiight, so why did you call me and ask about him?"

I pause before repeating, "He's just a friend, Mom."

I then hang up the phone, throwing it across the room and pulling out a book to try and distract myself.

The following month is simultaneously the shortest and the longest of my life. In some ways, I feel like time is flying by, but at the same time, I spend all of my time daydreaming and overthinking, so the days also feel like they are dragging by.

I try to distract myself with good books and walks on the beach, sketchpad in hand. But drawing the crashing waves and reading about happily ever afters doesn't take my mind off Stephan coming to visit. Feeling like I'm back in kindergarten, I realize that all of my sketches are either of Stephan or his name. Truly, am I a child again? Am I in love with someone who is basically a stranger?

I spend my days and nights scrolling through his photos on Facebook. Just to be prepared. As a friend, of course.

I go to church and have my head bowed in prayer for

most of the sermon, to the extent that I barely hear a whisper of what is said or any of the songs that are sung. After the service, I go to the personal reflection room and continue to pray by myself for several hours, but I can't shake the nerves.

The next week, one of the partners at my firm asks me to mentor Owen, showing him the ropes on how to use our CRM and teaching him where to go to review case law. After this frustrating interaction, Owen acts as if he were self-taught on something I had taught him about building charts and graphs in a staff meeting. The other partner praises him, saying that he knew his choice in hiring Owen would pay off. I escape into a daydream. My career is a good choice for me and fulfilling overall, but at times it can be very frustrating. Sometimes I feel like being a woman in this field is an uphill battle. Despite this, I always feel understood by Stephan online.

A few days before he's scheduled to arrive, I wake up to three missed calls from an unknown number. I ignore this, assuming some teenagers were playing a prank, but a sense of unease starts to stir beneath the surface. I don't have many numbers blocked, but the possibility of it being one person makes me nervous.

The morning of his arrival, I spend nearly an hour in the shower, compared to my usual 5-7 minutes. I am so nervous that I hold on to the support beam to avoid falling and hurting myself. After I'm convinced that I smell an acceptable level of fine, I throw all of the clothes from my walk-in closet onto the floor, unable to decide what to wear. I have dated and been involved with men my entire life, and yet I've never been as stressed as I am in preparing to meet Stephan again. But I've never been as excited, either.

* * *

8 pm. Stephan's flight lands in two hours. He caught the last flight out of San Antonio, having driven there from what essentially became his hometown of Alpine, Texas. Not as cool as Marfa from what I've heard, but close enough. He's visiting me "as a friend," and we haven't seen each other in person since we were little kids. I have liked him since we first started talking again as adults but have never admitted that to him. When we have random chats over social media on a weekend or late in the evening, I assume that he likes me too, but I have never had the guts to tell him how I feel. And now he's visiting.

I take the bus to meet him at the airport. He's getting a rental car for ease of use, but I had wanted to meet him there. Twenty minutes until his flight lands. I am nervous. Breathe in, breathe out. Breathe in, breathe out.

While walking to find my seat on the bus, I notice a peculiar old man with an oval-shaped face and receding hairline. He is pouring over a magazine one-handedly and behaving very strangely. Realizing he was rubbing himself through his jeans, I attempt to get to my seat until the bus jerks and I fall backward slightly. He drops his magazine, pages filled with provocative content, and smiling widely, asks, "Do I inspire you, ma'am?"

Grossed out and vowing to never become like this man, and ideally never be inspired by him either—except perhaps as an inspiration to do better—I try to get my mind off this and select a seat near the back exit. Only a few stops and a few minutes until I'm at the airport, and my friend's plane will land.

I get off the bus, quickly glancing behind me to ensure I am not being followed. Then, Stephan's flight lands. I stand waiting by baggage claim and see the flight from San Antonio appear on baggage drop four. I see him coming out of the secure area. "Phoebe?" he says, as we start closing the distance. What do I do? He's just a friend. I try not to second-guess myself and run up to him with my arms wide open. He picks me up and spins me, saying, "Long time no see." I feel a tingling throughout my whole body, with a strong pull that makes me feel like I want to dive off a diving board into open water.

Awkwardly, I tell him that he looks great, and then I feel I can't make eye contact. He tells me that I look great, too, and then awkward silence ensues.

He hadn't scheduled the showing to see me, right? Charleston is an artsy enough town for it to be a coincidence. I had offered him my couch for his trip. To save money, you know?

He takes me to pick up his rental car, and we make awkward, stilted small talk. "So, how's the weather? Oh, right, we're in the same place," I say. He chuckles, maybe thinking I said it as a joke. I mentally face-palm at this awkward question, but I truly wasn't expecting to see him in the flesh again. I had thought we were just the modern equivalent of pen pals.

He drives us to my neighborhood, and I show him where the guest parking is before giving him a quick tour of my home. While neither of us is the biggest fan of TV or movies, we sit on the couch and rewatch a movie about dinosaurs that we had seen together as little kids. We are sitting on opposite sides of the couch with my legs on top of his, but he couldn't possibly mean anything by letting me do this, I think to myself. I just don't have an ottoman. I'll have to buy one at some point soon, to avoid people feeling compelled to make near-romantic gestures due to the limited space allotted.

The movie finishes without much fanfare.

As I get up from the couch, intending to go to bed, Stephan says "Phoebe, there's something I've been meaning to tell you..." I am instantly worried that he will tell me that he doesn't like me as more than a friend or that I will accidentally admit my feelings, so I avoid the conversation entirely. Perhaps not the best choice.

"Have a nice night," I say before shutting my bedroom door. The next morning, he is nowhere to be found. Did I scare him off? Maybe I should have listened to what he had to say.

He pops back into my sunny rented townhome a few minutes later. "I grabbed myself a coffee and you some peppermint tea with stevia. Your favorite, right?" I stand there, surprised and in awe, grateful that he remembered a one-off comment I made six months ago. Yes, I love peppermint tea and drink it frequently. I had some in my cabinet, though, but I know he is just being nice. As a friend.

He then pulls a book out of a bag, saying that he remembered I liked to read fantasy books, and the coffee shop had some indie books for sale. It was a thin paper-back book with a purple cover, featuring a goose. *The*

Ever-Dark by El Hoffman, it read. "The lady at the register said it's been all the rage lately. Apparently, it's a character-driven fantasy novella, so I thought you'd love it."

I thank him, as fantasy is one of my favorite genres, and I had never been able to leave the house without at least one book.

He then follows up, saying he had purchased a poetry book that he thought would inspire his artwork, *The Pirate, The Pen & The Flame: A Collection of Poems by Pat Ulacco*. Apparently, Pat is a poet who lives by the beach up in North Carolina, and his collection has been flying off the shelves nearly as fast as the fantasy book. He opens the book, claiming he had read an interesting poem while in line to pay:

"Dream well, dream real,
trust what you feel.
We saw no mermaids
but the magic
was still present in
every
stroke
of
the pen.
And when
I think
about it,
she
must have
been there too."

Extremely perplexed as to why he would pick this poem to read, I say that I thought it was interesting and would need to flip through the other poems at some point. I am just more of a fantasy or romance reader than a poetry person.

Coffee in hand and having set the book down, he puts on a 2010s cover of a classic 80s slow song, sensual and steady, backed by a saxophone and 4/4 timing, but with a crisper tone and more rhythm and percussion than the original. This cover is almost punchy, rather than being smooth jazz. I love this song and listen to it frequently! Feeling comfortable, I begin to dance around the kitchen.

After the song is over, he seemingly decides that he has had enough of other music and pulls a ukulele out of his bag. I didn't know he played the ukulele. He asks if I'd like to go sit on my patio. We gaze out at the pastel rooftops, lining the way to the Atlantic shoreline. We can just barely see the crashing waves, and we are not making eye contact. I'm too nervous to look at him, and he's giving off nervous energy as well. His hands are tracing circles on the iron balcony railing, and the tension in the air is palpable. He soon breaks the silence. "Do you know of a good place for shrimp and grits?" he asks. "I've always wanted to try them."

I respond, "I don't eat dairy, and I've heard most places use butter. But I could go for some shrimp."

He responds, "Did you know that some mantis shrimp exhibit monogamous behavior? While they don't mate for life like penguins, I have a lot of respect for them because of that."

At this point, I look at him quizzically, and he immediately looks away and starts tuning his ukulele. He starts playing one of my favorite songs on his ukulele, one from an indie band originally from Portland, Oregon. He quietly sings along as well, which makes me start wishing he were truly serenading me and not just playing and singing in the presence of an old friend.

He puts his ukulele back in the case inside, and we decide to go take a stroll on the beach, but I feel the need to avoid touching him or making direct eye contact as he's just a friend. He tells me how pretty my blonde hair looks in the sunlight and that I look radiant with the sun shining on my face. Then, "beautiful," he remarks. But he's an artist. These types of comments must be typical for him, I reason to myself. I assume that I must be no different from a wild duck in a pond to him.

After this, we head to lunch, and he pays for both of our meals. He has the budget for this. No other reason, I rationalize. He told me he's not actually a starving artist. I remember his "jk" in true internet fashion. The tension in the air is still palpable, and I believe I catch him glancing at me a time or two.

After lunch, I introduce him to my favorite bakery in town—fully vegan and gluten-free, yet you would never know it. When the bell dings, announcing that customers have entered, the older woman manning the register incorrectly states that we look like such a cute couple. "She's dressed so beautifully for you. I hope you'll pay for her sweets. How long have you been together?" she asks. We both start speaking at the same time, cutting each other off. "Oh, we're not together," I finally manage to say. The woman responds disbelievingly, with a simple "uh-huh."

We both get cream-filled, chocolate frosted donuts and pain au chocolate—he corrects me after I refer to them as "chocolate croissants." Artists, man. They know way too much about pastries.

When we get back to my place from lunch, ready to play a round of a racing video game on the TV like we did in kindergarten, something almost completely unexpected happens. Amelia, my ex-girlfriend from many years ago, is standing at the front door. Oh no. "Amelia, what are you doing here? I thought you were married! Shouldn't you be with your husband instead of awkwardly hovering at your ex-girlfriend's door?"

"No, no. He hurt me, and I have nowhere else to go... so I was hoping I could stay here."

"Can't you stay with your mother, or literally anyone else? You surely must still have friends, or at least money for a bed in a hotel somewhere. Right?"

"No, I have nowhere else to go, and no money...please take me in. I'm separating from my husband and am going to divorce him again. He's not a good man."

"In the nicest way possible, Amelia, why does this concern me? Why are you here? What makes you think I'd take you back or even take you in? You left me for this man, and now you want to leave him for me? I'm not a revolving door. Please leave."

"Please just let me stay here for the night. I promise I'll leave in the morning, and you'll never see me again come daybreak. Please just let me stay here for the night. Or maybe we could go take a stroll on the beach, walk into the water, chat..." she says. Amelia then notices the man standing beside me. "Wait, who are you? You were single last I checked through someone's phone on Facebook, so why is a guy here, Phoebe?"

"You little manipulator. I do not want to take a stroll on the beach. You left me for a man, and now you're leaving him and coming back to my front door. This is not happening. Please go!"

At this point, Stephan butts in, saying, "C'mon, she has nowhere else to go. Just let her stay the night. She can sleep on the couch."

"And where would you sleep?"

"You have a walk-in closet, right? I guess I'll sleep on the floor like a puppy, if you'll let me." "This is ridiculous, and both of you need to leave. I'm not a charity. I'm not a women's shelter. I'm not a backup plan or plan B. I'm not a revolving door. I'm not a doormat. I'm not a dumpster. And I'm not falling for this again."

"Why do I need to leave?"

"Because I'm not falling prey to Amelia's mind games again. It's always a slippery slope with her. First, she's on the couch, and then she's telling everyone how much she loves me, and I fall for her games and traps again. I have no interest in spending time with anyone who entertains her."

"Fine," he says, but I can see and feel the pain and what almost looks like heartbreak in Stephan's eyes as he turns to leave.

Stephan and Amelia both leave, hopefully separately. I regret kicking him out almost immediately and feel a pain in my chest, but I have a zero-tolerance policy where Amelia is concerned. She left me to get back together with her abusive ex-husband, claiming that despite him destroying her life, no one else would love him, so she had to. While I feel a deep sympathy for her, she is not my responsibility.

I haven't heard from her since kicking her off my front porch this afternoon, but I don't have the time or the mental energy to deal with her or anyone who sides with her. As I told Stephan, I'm not a charity.

Part Two

I pace across the room. Back and forth, I can't move past what had just happened. I pick back up the books Stephan had bought, and flipping through the poetry book, I go back to wondering why he read me that poem in particular. Quietly laughing despite the pain, I ponder if he knew what he has been doing to me. "Does he know how I feel?" I think to myself.

I try to forget about it. Fuming, I call Bryan, the accountant I had gone out with the other night.

Over the next few weeks, I go on three more dates with Bryan, perhaps out of spite, but I just can't get my mind off Stephan. I had not bothered to unfollow him or unfriend him, but I did mute him and prevent him from viewing my stories. This means I have no idea what has happened or where he has been since then—I just hope deep inside of myself that Amelia didn't convince him to date her after she realized I wasn't an option. I can't let this take up too much mental energy, though, so I start reading *The Ever-Dark*, and maybe relating a little too much to the protagonist, Violet. I begin really wishing I could meet one of the side characters, a pedicab driver named Kazuki, for even just a moment. He seems to always be more in tune with reality than I ever have been and probably ever will be, and it often feels like he can read minds, especially that of the main character. If only he could tell me how Stephan feels, I think to myself. I continue reading, and as the room begins to be filled with darkness, I get to a scene where the love interest makes a mistake, and I have to set the book aside for the night. "I hope that will never happen to me," I whisper softly to myself.

* * *

The next day, I go for a swim in the ocean, and walking along the beach afterwards, I end up at the restaurant where Stephan and I had gotten lunch that one day. Shrimp and grits, he had had. I continue trying to convince myself I am over him, but I end up gazing up at a mural of two geese while sipping a virgin pina colada. I feel terrible grief, and I miss him very badly.

This prompts me to call Katarina. I try to separate business and my personal life for the most part, but as she is a newlywed, I thought she might have insight that I don't. The next day, after I get out of church, we meet up at a local breakfast spot for biscuits and gravy, mine dairy-free and with all the fixings. I give her an overview of everything that has ever happened with Stephan. "He clearly likes you, Phoebe. You shouldn't chase a man like that away. Why don't you just call him?" But I didn't believe what she was telling me.

Four more months pass, and after making bad decisions like going out with Bryan, I learn that I need to fly to Michigan for work. My client in Blissfield, Michigan needs a construction and zoning inspection done where a drunk driver crashed into their house. The homeowners are suing the town for zoning negligence. All expenses of the trip are covered. One of the partners, Owen, and I are all going, but I was told this is going to be a major test of my skill set.

My late grandparents had lived in Michigan, and I often spent summers with them, so I am intimately familiar with Blissfield and had planned to pick up a donut or two while in town. I love late summer bleeding into early fall in Southeastern Michigan and thought this would be a good experience to distract myself from Stephan.

I bought a tablet with a stylus and started marking a tally every time I thought of him. A kind person in my past had taught me this tactic to stop doing or thinking of something you'd like to move past, and unfortunately, a very long scroll in my notetaking software was full of tally marks. It functioned a lot like a swear jar, in a way.

Before heading into Blissfield for the business trip, I drive into the cemetery where my grandparents are buried, wanting to talk to them a bit and pray for a few minutes. I get down on my knees and kiss their headstones, as I always do. "Grandma, Grandpa. I am not sure what to do. Do you remember Stephan, my old best friend? I'm obsessed with him. I love him. I just keep telling myself that I don't, and he's just a friend. I don't know if he feels the same or if I'm overthinking everything and reading way too far into every interaction we have. I kicked him out because he sided with my ex-girlfriend, and I still feel so much regret over it. I wish I could tell him the truth, but I don't know if I'll ever have another opportunity." Sobbing, I put my head in my hands until a cool breeze brushed over my shoulders, and I felt that my grandparents were there with me.

"I wish you could have been there when I got my JD. I'm terrified to take the Bar Exam. I don't want to risk my pride by failing and needing to retake it like my driver's test. The Lord knows I still can't parallel park, and I don't want law to become like that for me, too," I sob.

For a moment, I swear I hear my grandma laughing, and then another breeze blows over my shoulders. At this point, I was able to stand up and take a few deep breaths before touching their headstones and saying goodbye.

Although I had tear-stained glasses, I felt like I was in a better place. I ran into the small chain grocery store in nearby Adrian to grab some cold brew and a box of peppermint tea. After thinking of him and completing yet another set of five tallies, there he was in the flesh. It's him, the dreaded almost-one, friend-not-friend, will-they-won't-they. Stephan stood ten feet ahead of me, grabbing a bag of plain salted potato chips off the shelf.

"What are you *doing* here? You live in Texas. Why are you in Southeastern Michigan of all places?"

"Oh, well, I heard about this sprawling oak tree off the road in a field that people like to park under sometimes. I had wanted to paint it, and it convinced me to fly out. I also heard about this collection of pine trees nearby, and I was planning to sketch those with some oil pastels tomorrow. But that isn't important, why are you here?" Glancing at my tablet, still in hand, he continues, "and what's with all those tally marks? Were you locked up somewhere?" he asks, and he knowingly raises one of his eyebrows.

"For work...I'm investigating a house that is across the street from a dead end. Some guy blew through the stop sign, crashing into their dining room. They're suing the town for zoning reasons, claiming they shouldn't have been sold a house across the street from a stop sign. I need to be on site for the construction inspection and be on hand for any questions as needed," I say.

He shakes his head, as if he doesn't believe my excuse. I wasn't being dishonest per se, but that definitely wasn't the reason for the tallies, and he appears to know this.

He asks me if I want to grab food with him, and (not using my best judgment), I agree and suggest a local burger place.

When we arrive, he tells me that he has missed me and apologizes for upsetting me, while I pour an uncommonly large amount of mustard onto my pretzel bun. He admits he still doesn't quite understand the issue with Amelia.

Of course, he must miss me as a friend and not in an obsessive way.

"She destroyed my life, Stephan. We're talking about a woman who lied to my face and left me for her ex-husband that I thought she had stopped speaking to... all while I had loved her and was thinking about proposing. I was young and didn't know I deserved better, yet. I have no interest in having her in my life, and I don't want to entertain anyone who seems to side with her," I say with despair lacing my tone.

What appears like sadness is visible in his eyes when he replies, "I don't side with her, though. I only knew you had a 'crazy' ex named Amelia who had left you out of nowhere, but I wasn't aware of the specifics. Maybe I should have asked, but I don't often discuss my exes, so I had assumed it was a sore subject. I didn't mean to make you upset or angry. I had only intended to suggest we put some kindness out in the world for a night. I have long since realized that I overstepped and that it was not my place to suggest she stay with you, as it was your home and I was merely a visitor. She tried to hit on me as soon as we were out of sight, which didn't sit well with me. You were right," he says. He continues, "Honestly, have you thought about getting a restraining order? You work in law, and I'm sure you could win the case if you tried. Then I'd be safe from her clutches as well, I hope. Though I haven't heard from her since I drove away and left her quite literally in the dust."

For a moment, I feel unable to process everything he said, but then I realize that he doesn't want to lose me. As a friend. I need to be careful to avoid admitting my feelings.

He shakes his head and starts eating his sweet potato fries. "What have you been up to lately? Other than the one that brought you out here, have you been involved with any interesting cases?"

"Not particularly." I take a bite of my food, some mustard dripping onto the plate—a perfect built-in dipping sauce for my fries.

Stephan glances over and chuckles. "Just like old times, you were always my favorite mustard girl."

Right, I think to myself. As Clara always preferred ketchup. No other reason.

I continue, "I am often subjected to research and

supportive roles, as I haven't taken the Bar Exam yet. While I finished my JD with a 4.0 in the spring, I don't want to fail the Bar like I did my driver's test the first time – stupid traffic cones, I still can't parallel park."

He says that his last art showing in North Charleston went well and that he was considering doing another in three months or so. He asks if he can stay with me again, clarifying that he can still sleep on the couch unless I would truly prefer the closet, but that he'd specifically be scheduling the art showing to see me this time, as he wants to reconnect with me.

"We were such great childhood friends," he says, and adds that he doesn't have any good excuses other than that he made a mistake in not trusting my judgment with Amelia, and not getting to know me when he still had the time.

More evidence that he only likes me as a friend; he quite literally just emphasized that we were childhood friends.

Late into the evening, I continue my denial, trying to convince myself that I don't actually like him and feeling as if I know full well that he doesn't like me romantically.

The next day, after a grueling 9 hours of inspections and research, Stephan picks me up, and then he parks his rental under the tree he had mentioned. Of course, he probably just wants another set of eyes on his next art piece. After a few minutes of awkward conversation in his car, he asks me if I'd like to go sit under the tree on some towels he brought. Multiple towels. Because we are friends, I rationalize. No other reason.

We sit on our separate but almost touching towels, and he begins to paint the tree with his rental car under it. I pick up my copy of the latest in a 12-book-long series of Christian small-town romance books when I receive a text. My phone buzzes far too loudly for the quiet serenity of the field, and Stephan asks who the message is from.

"Just a guy I went on a few dates with recently," I hesitantly reply.

Before I can finish my train of thought, he responds with "Oh."

Trying to finish my sentence, I quickly respond with unintentional uptalk in my tone, "I'm not interested in him, I've been meaning to tell him that. I hate to say this or even think like this, but he was just a distraction. I'm going to let him know that I'm not interested, and while I wish him the best, he won't hear from me again."

Stephan doesn't respond, but he gulps loudly before returning to his painting. I hope he doesn't understand what I meant by distraction, unless he feels the same way. But I know he doesn't.

When I glance over a few minutes later, I notice that a woman lying down on a picnic blanket has made it onto the canvas. "Is that me?" I scooch over and ask, while approaching his separate towel. "But I'm not on a picnic blanket, I'm on a towel!" I exclaim.

"Well, you are here. Are you not?" he responds.

"I guess I am," I respond. Maybe I'm too literal of a thinker when it comes to artistic expression, but I know his drawing of me doesn't mean anything. Artists draw people all the time. My shape must have just been needed to balance out the picture—no other reason.

At that moment, his phone buzzes as mine had a few minutes ago. "It's just Clara. She wanted me to tell you she says hi," he says.

"Your sister knows you're with me right now?" I respond.

"Of course she does. Why wouldn't she? Actually, let me show you something…" he says, and then he pulls out his wallet and removes a picture. He passes it to me, saying, "Here."

It was a picture of him, his sister, and me when we were all little kids. It was taken around the time his sister had mentioned wishing that we were sisters. Clara is a few years older and was holding me, and Stephan was sitting next to us with a smile so big it nearly touched his ears.

I tear up slightly, and ask, "You still have this? And you keep it in your wallet – why?"

"It's one of my favorite memories, and both of my favorite people together in one photo. I really wish we could have stayed in touch, Phoebe. I still wonder what might've happened."

He pauses before asking, "Actually, I've wanted to ask you something. When I was walking around earlier, I noticed that a branch of my church back home is having a dance tonight. It's not too far from here. Would you like to go with me? And maybe tomorrow we can go check out those pine trees?"

"Of course, I'm so glad you remember me mentioning I like to dance," and then I laugh before continuing, "I actually went to the grove of pine trees with a guy I dated in my early twenties, when I visited my grandparents for a few weeks. They're beautiful. Honestly, I had no words for how lovely the experience was." I mentally face-palm after mentioning yet another guy I had dated in his presence. I feel like I seriously need to get myself together.

He seemingly doesn't want to touch on the second half of what I said because he responds, "I don't just remember you saying you liked to dance, Phoebe. I remember the two of us in kindergarten, dancing to 'Macarena' at that one school dance. Remember? You were wearing a blue and purple dress, and you fell. I helped you get back up so that we could finish dancing, and Mrs. Kennedy made a comment about how we'd get married one day. Fun times," he says. He then follows up with, "And you literally danced in your kitchen when I came to visit. Don't you remember the saxophone?"

"Yes, I love the song you played in the kitchen. And oh, well, I still like dancing to 'Macarena.' I'd be down to go tonight, that sounds fun. Do you think they'll play 'Macarena'?" I ask, while daydreaming about what could happen at the dance if he feels the way I do. But of course, there's no way he does. He only mentioned the dance and the marriage comment because he saw those flyers for the dance tonight.

He laughs and says, "If they don't, I'll have to request it."

After he finishes his painting and I'm about halfway through my book, he remarks that we should probably get ready. He drops me off where I'm staying and says he'll be back in an hour. I only have business clothing and a sundress, though. I didn't think to bring anything dance-appropriate or formal attire. I settle for my blue sundress, which modestly covers my shoulders (as all my clothing does). I then put a black blazer over it to make it a bit dressier. I had just finished putting in my sterling silver dangling earrings when I hear a knock at the door.

He's there to pick me up, wearing black dress pants with a dark grey button-up long-sleeved shirt. Seemingly at random, he says, "I have a question for you, Phoebe."

Taken aback, I respond hesitatingly, "Okay?"

"So, the church I go to encourages sobriety, which I know is an important value of yours as well. I wanted to let you know that I used to drink alcohol, but I stopped a few years ago. I hope that doesn't bother you and isn't a deal-breaker," he says with possible uncertainty lacing his words.

"I think that was a statement and not a question, but no – why would that bother me? I used to drink as well," I respond. And a dealbreaker for what? I think to myself. Ah, friendship!

After a brief pause, I continue speaking, "My industry is very alcohol-dominated—being sober is unexpected and maybe even unusual, but yes, it's important to me. While professional colleagues or clients drinking doesn't bother me, I prefer to surround myself with people who don't drink," I respond.

We arrive at the church, and a giant picture of Jesus greets us at the door. I consider myself a Protestant, so this is a bit unexpected yet welcome. I had never thought to display the Son of God so overtly, but after pondering it for a minute, I begin to believe that more churches should do so. I feel I could get on board with some aspects of this denomination.

"M'lady," he says before extending his arm out to me, seemingly expecting me to link my arm with his. But we are just there to do the Macarena, and this isn't a date, I remind myself before crossing my arms and looking away.

He sighs, and I can't put my finger on why, but we continue onward to the church's gymnasium, complete with both a stage and basketball hoops. What a wonder. It looks so much like our childhood school's gym. For a moment, I find myself caught up in the memory.

When we walk into the large room, I notice that disco balls hang from the ceiling, and some of the tables laid out along the walls have miniature disco balls in vases. I love disco balls, and one of my favorite songs mentions them, so this feels like a wonderful occasion already.

Without a cue, "Macarena" starts playing, causing me to run to the dance floor, ready to dance. Just like I did in kindergarten, I fell, but without the pliability of a child's body. I was very much looking forward to the night, but unlike in kindergarten, I sprain my ankle. "Ouch!" I cry out, and the evening takes an unexpected turn as Stephan must take me to urgent care to get my ankle looked at. This derails the following day's plans as well, and I end up needing to fly home early and rest, as my insurance chose to fight me over needing an ankle scooter. Unfortunately, I cannot finish the inspections without two working legs. Stephan wishes me well at the airport, needing to return both of our rental cars somehow, and then I fly home. "I'll see you in three months?" he asks, continuing with, "For the art showing?"

"With my clumsiness, my ankle will probably still have me down for the count, so I don't think I'll be anywhere else. Just let me know when you'll be in town, and I'll be around," I say, wishing very deeply within myself that he could be more than a friend.

* * *

After a 3-hour flight delay followed by a bumpy flight, I manage to get inside my townhome, and I collapse into bed, wishing I would have had the urge to tell Stephan that I like him before my ankle threw everything off. "I could just tell him," I briefly think, but I worry that sending such a text would only mess things up, and I don't want to lose him as a friend like I almost did after Amelia's stunt.

Over the next few weeks, my ankle slowly heals, and I end up passing the Bar Exam on my first attempt. My coworkers throw me a huge party, and Stephan video chats in as I asked him to. For moral support, of course. I feel extremely grateful to have reached this point in my life, as there was once a time when I never thought I would even make it to my high school graduation. And now I'm a fully-fledged lawyer!

The day after my party, I get a text from Clara, having not heard from her except through Stephan in about 20 years. "Congratulations on passing the Bar, and I hope your ankle is doing better. You should come visit us sometime. I miss you." Friendly words between childhood friends. I respond, "I miss you too. Stephan is coming to visit in a few months. You could always come too! I'm not sure I have room for two guests, though."

Clara responds, "Haha, I think I'll leave you and Stephan to it this time, but definitely come visit me sometime. Don't be a stranger," she says.

What is that supposed to mean? I like the message, and then toss my phone across the room yet again, grateful for the carpet in my townhome's master bedroom. I don't want to order yet another replacement screen protector, yet I stubbornly refuse to stop the behavior.

After all of this time, I continue believing there is nothing between Stephan and me. His liking my posts, stories, and videos within minutes and responding warmly to messages, and even sending a few warm messages of his own, doesn't mean he likes me the way I like him. Yet, I continue to be grateful that he doesn't post pictures with women other than Clara, and his Facebook relationship status continues reading "single." The dance invite and his admitting his next trip would just be to see me couldn't mean anything, right? Artistic people are just very flowery like I am, I reason.

Part Three

Three months after the Michigan trip, as promised, Stephan flies into Charleston for another art showing of his. When I meet him at the airport this time, he acts extremely nervous and off-kilter. Very unlike him, despite the social anxiety he once mentioned having been diagnosed with when he was in middle school. He sleeps on the couch that night, and the next day, I drive us to the art gallery in North Charleston. He gratefully gave me a free ticket, so I didn't need to worry about paying. Truthfully, though, I had wanted to support him monetarily. While he acts as a salesman, trying to sell his paintings to the highest bidder, I walk around and admire his artwork. Beautiful sea turtle paintings, the painting he did of me under the tree in Michigan, quite a few of red barns, seemingly in Texas, and many other works adorn the walls, causing me to become more and more impressed with him. As a friend.

At one point, I glance over at Stephan and see another woman laughing at something he said. I know that he's working and is probably pitching a sale of a piece, and I know that we aren't together, but it rubs me the wrong way, causing me to briefly step outside for some air. After a few minutes, I go back inside, but he stops me just inside the entrance. "Hey, there you are, I was looking for you!" he says with an uplifted tone and seemingly nervous and slightly shaky smile. Now that the art showing is over, he appears more nervous, with his hands visibly shaking. He asks, "I have something I'd like to show you. Are you down for a road trip tonight?"

"Tonight?" I ask warily, knowing I had planned to finish the book I was currently reading tonight.

"Yeah, I'd really like to show you something in Georgia, and we can head back on Sunday," he clarifies.

"We have to go all the way to Georgia? Can't you just show me a picture?" I ask, not understanding the sudden urge to take a road trip.

"Trust me, you'll love it," he says, but I feel doubtful that I could love anything other than my book tonight. Unless he wanted me to love him? Surely not.

We go back and pack our bags for our weekend trip, and he agrees to drive the whole way without music on, so I can finish reading my book. I'm very grateful for this, at least. He finds us a nice chain hotel off the highway in the far northern suburbs of Atlanta, and he gets us a room with two queen beds. Because we're friends, I surmise. Or maybe there was only one room left. Or maybe he just can't afford two rooms, despite not truly being a starving artist. He probably feels bad having asked me to go on this last-minute jaunt across state lines, and I'm grateful he isn't expecting me to sleep in his rental car.

The night passes by very slowly, and I struggle to sleep. Late at night, I wake from a dream about the two of us and Clara as children. We were all chasing each other on the playground, back when everything felt as it was supposed to. Before my people were taken away from me.

I look at the clock and see that it reads 3 am. At this point, I became very tempted to crawl into Stephan's bed, but I know it would cause more problems than it is worth. At this point, I fall into a fitful sleep, and around 8 am, I struggle to feel like I didn't wake up on the wrong side of the bed—or in the wrong bed.

After having coffee in the hotel breakfast nook in the morning, we check out, with him claiming we would need to stay elsewhere tonight and would make a longer drive back tomorrow—all on his dime, of course. Because he feels bad for asking me to follow his whims, I'm sure. No other reason.

We get on the highway, with his phone propped up in a GPS holder mounted to the dash. For a moment, Clara's name appears on the screen. "You're really doing it? I'm so happy to hear that," the text reads. Uncertain about what she means by that, I begin to feel nervous with the sensation of my heart in my throat. I choose not to mention the message, and Stephan doesn't appear to notice his phone went off to begin with.

* * *

After 45 minutes or so on the road, he drives into a small town and parks in a parking lot of what appears to be an outdoor mall with a ton of green space. "C'mon," he says to me.

We walk for a few minutes, and he begins to slow as we approach what I believe is a Middle Eastern restaurant, given the mural and neon sign, most likely remaining off until nighttime, that says "I Falafel You" with a heart around the words.

"I'm confused—you drove me to the Atlanta suburbs to get Middle Eastern food? I live a few doors down from a great falafel restaurant in Charleston, and we could have gone there. Or even some frozen or homemade falafel would have been great," I say. I have a nearly full bag of frozen falafel and some eggplant dip in my freezer as we speak, after all!

"No, Phoebe...I brought you here because I painted this mural, and they based the sign off of it as well," he explains.

"It's a beautiful mural, but I still don't think I understand. I knew you were talented, but is the food really worth the nearly 5-hour drive one way with traffic?" I respond, questioning his meaning.

"No. I mean yes, but no, that's not why I brought us here. After the encounter with Amelia and all that transpired, I was offered this project by someone at the art showing I did in North Charleston. I drove out here for it, and the name of the restaurant really reminded me of how I feel about you," he remarks.

I begin tearing up, saying, "I don't understand, why would a heartfelt mural remind you of your childhood friend? Or is it because the word falafel is so close to 'laugh' and you find me funny?" I ask, before continuing and mentally putting my tongue in my mouth, "Or maybe I'm just dense, like some falafel is?" I respond, beginning to understand that maybe there has been another reason.

Clarifying, he says, "Let's please stop beating around the bush, okay? Phoebe, I've loved you ever since we were children, and these past few years I've had so many instances where I should've told you, but I was always so nervous, not believing you felt the same way. But I know you do, Phoebe. Anyone can tell by the way you look at me, and by the cryptic things you say. I was offered a position as the head of an art museum in Austin, and I'm really excited about the opportunity. Not only would I run the museum, but they would be adding a wing for my artwork, and I would have the opportunity to teach art classes as well. It's something that makes me want to settle down, and..."

I interrupt him, "Austin, where? Austin, Texas? What's in Austin other than the role?" I ask, while wishing he were telling me that he wants to move back to Charleston instead of elsewhere in Texas, and still continuing to reason that he loves me as a friend, or perhaps as a sister, like Clara had said back when we were kids.

"Well, hopefully you, Phoebe. I would love for you to come to Austin with me. I know it doesn't have a beach, but it has some beautiful lakes that made me think of you." He then gets down on one knee, and pulls out a 14k yellow gold, 2mm band, 1 carat oval diamond ring, exactly what I had dreamed of my entire life. Then he asks, "I should have asked you this many moons ago, but I want to spend my life with you. Will you marry me, Phoebe?"

Visibly shaking and feeling like I had been as dense as

falafel for the past few years, I respond without hesitation. "Of course I will, Stephan. This whole time, I've lived in denial, hoping you had liked me as well, but I was never sure if the feeling was mutual. I always rationalized that your behavior was just because you cared deeply for me as a friend, as Clara did."

He picks me up and spins me around as before, but this time, after he sets me down, he slips the ring on my left ring finger and kisses me deeply for the first time. I lean into him and finally feel as if all the puzzle pieces are metaphorically falling into place. After a few minutes of holding each other, we go into the restaurant, and as the bell dings to alert our arrival, the servers express gratitude for Stephan's visit.

We then order a side of hummus with pita and kalamata olives, as well as two falafel wraps with fries to celebrate. Our server comps our meal, due to Stephan having blessed their building with his artwork, as well as our newfound engagement.

* * *

The week after Stephan flies home, I talk to the partners in my firm. I express gratitude for the time I worked there, as well as bittersweetness for the need to leave. Unfortunately, I won't be able to work my way up to partner any longer, and I choose to put in an extended notice ahead of my move to Texas. There will be a few hoops I will need to jump through over the next few months to move my licensure across state lines, but I feel ready to begin my forever with Stephan, and I know it will all be worth it in the end.

Epilogue (Clara's POV)

Driving to Phoebe's church this morning, I couldn't contain my excitement. I had always hoped that Stephan and Phoebe would get married, but I never thought the day would come. Stephan and I are LDS, so they opted to have a wedding at Phoebe's church rather than have a civil wedding. As is typical in our faith, they opted for a quick engagement, lasting only three months. I am grateful to have been asked to be both the maid of honor and the best woman, and I have a feeling this will be one of the best days of my life. Phoebe, my best childhood friend, will finally be my sister!

I pull up to her church building in my yellow VW Beetle, wearing a long-sleeved, knee-length, blue and grey floral dress. After getting out of the car and walking around the building, I see that the back grounds have already been prepared for the festivities, full of fake blue freesias as Phoebe is allergic to flower pollen.

When the ceremony begins, I start to cry tears of joy. Phoebe looks beautiful in her long white gown, which has flowy sleeves, a high neckline, and a fully covered back, with small embroidered blue flowers in a few places along the bottom hem—seemingly as the "something blue," as well as matching the freesias. My brother looks just as stunning, truly handsome beyond measure, in a medium-to-dark grey tuxedo with a faux blue flower pinned above his heart, most likely intending to match her.

As they are announced as man and wife, I start to daydream about the potential of meeting "the one" as well. Maybe someday.

Still Waters

The next morning, Phoebe and Stephan wake up in their shared bed together, and for once, Phoebe feels peace in her life. No more uncertainty, no more confusion. Just the one she is meant to be with, and hopefully some peppermint tea.

"Meant to Be"

I feel as if
I am floating in the sea
I never knew love
Until you met me

Acknowledgments

I would like to thank Heather Hoffman-Seifert, Kate Ashford, and Emma Snapp for supporting me as initial readers. I would also like to thank Sam Bolano for his work as my illustrator.

Additionally, I would like to thank my former English professor Kevin Jett for acting as my proofreader. Kevin, your support has always been invaluable—thank you for your continued faith in me.

I'm also thankful for Pat Ulacco, whose original poem and likeness appear in this book with his permission. His contribution helped shape *No Other Reason*, and I am immensely grateful. If you enjoyed the included poem, you might appreciate his published poetry as well.

Last but not least, thank you to my readers for allowing my vision to take root in your minds. I hope you enjoyed *No Other Reason* and its included poems. If you did, please consider leaving a review on Amazon and/or Goodreads.

About the Author

El Hoffman (born February 8, 2000) is an author, poet, and data expert. A lifelong writer, she debuted with the literary fantasy novella *The Ever-Dark*. The novelette *The Scarlet-Dawn* serves as its direct sequel. El is also the author of the contemporary romance novelette *No Other Reason* and three poetry collections: *The Mirror, The Mask, and All I Ask*; *The Moon, The Tide, and All I Tried*; and *The Volcano, The Flame, and All I Became*. Her work has also been featured in multiple anthologies.

Outside of fiction, El has built a career implementing HubSpot for businesses and earned her Master of Science in Data Analytics from Eastern University in 2024.

When she's not writing or working, she enjoys reading ebooks, taking long walks, and hula hooping. She's also passionate about video games, cooking, exploring new restaurants, and traveling.

instagram.com/elhoffmanauthor

amazon.com/author/elhoffman

tiktok.com/@elhoffmanauthor

bookbub.com/authors/el-hoffman

threads.com/@elhoffmanauthor

youtube.com/@elhoffmanauthor